ADVENTURES OF ALEX:

LEMONADE WARS

Lewis A. Howard

To order additional copies of this book, contact:
Xlibris
844-714-8691
www.Xlibris.com
Orders@Xlibris.com

ISBN: Softcover   978-1-6641-6700-1
        EBook   978-1-6641-6699-8

Print information available on the last page

Rev. date: 04/20/2021

ADVENTURES OF ALEX:

LEMONADE WARS

On this hot summer afternoon. I have my red swimming trunks on, sun tan lotion and my plastic blue star shaped sun glasses on. The sun is shining bright on my face. The sky is a light blue with no clouds. My mom wants to show me how to make Lemonade. It sounds really cool sitting in a swimming pool with a floating device while drinking lemonade. I started to sing l-e-m-o-n-a-d-e, lemonade in the summer. I watched my mom, she used four fresh lemons, half a cup of sugar, two quarts of water and ice. All in this one magic container with a spout. She placed it on the front porch and I say, the sugar was my favorite part. Although my mom don't allow me to eat a lot of sugar during the day. No candy bars, soda or kool aid.

She started to fill up my swimming pool and placed it in the front yard so, I could cool off. Then I heard screaming from a distance. The sound was getting louder and louder. I looked down the street and saw Sally running full speed. She was wearing a blue dress with football pads and no shoes. She reminded me of a caveman and I have to say, she could run over someone twice my size. She became closer and leaped towards my swimming pool, yelling my name in midair. Alex! Cannon ball! Sally splashed into the water. The sun disappeared for a short moment. A wave of water hit me. I stopped dead in my tracks with my mouth open. I started to shiver. I have to admit it was cold. Sally came up for air screaming with her arms above her head. Woot! Woot!

Wiping my eyes, I saw Eric on his skateboard. He was doing curb jumps and flip board tricks. Eric replied, "Hello Alex.", as he turned his head. Eric didn't see that big rock in front of him and ran into it. He flew right into a tree. He landed upside down. His body was in a U-shape and his helmet was covering his eyes as he stood up. He replied, "I'm ok", in a low tone voice as he stumbled across my front yard in a daze. I could see his skateboard was missing a wheel and his skateboard was cracked. Sally stood out of the water pointing at Eric and said, "That was like slow motion!" "Are you ok?" Eric replied, "Do you have anything to drink?" "I'm really thirsty." I said, "Sure." "My mom made some lemonade." "Would you like to try some?" "Yes please", Eric replied. I said, "Here, you can use my cup." Eric said, "That's nasty!" "I don't want to use the cup you drank out of!" "I might catch something or better yet, get sick!" "Germs yuck!" Sally said, "It would be like dropping my favorite ice cream on the ground!" "Picking it up and eating it!" "Disgusting!" Sally pulled Eric into the swimming pool with his clothes on and said, "Do you need to cool off?" We all started laughing. Splashing water everywhere. Eric was no longer concerned about his lemonade but never tried it.

Then across the street, we see the neighborhood bully selling lemonade for thirty cents a cup. The kids in the neighborhood was buying it. My mind began to wonder, what if I decide to sell it for 10 cents. I could get all of the kids to buy a lot of lemonade. I began to smile with greed and thought of one thing, money for the ice cream truck. I began to say, "Hey guys." "I have an idea." "What if, we sold my mom's lemonade?" "We could have money for the ice cream truck and share it." Sally and Eric agreed. Eric began to tap me on the shoulders and say, "Ah, Alex?" "Here comes Tommy, the neighborhood bully." We all trembled with fear except Sally. Tommy slowly begins to walk across the street looking both ways before he cross. Makes his way to the sidewalk and says, "My moms Lemonade is better than yours!" Yelling across the yard. I swallowed first before I spoke. My mom makes the best lemonade and I can prove it. At this time Sally was over my shoulders with her tongue hanging out on the left side of her mouth. Her eyes crossed growling like a mean dog. Tommy looked at her and ran back across the street yelling, this means war as he growled back. Eric looking on with his mouth open in amazement.

His eyes bulging out of his head. I began to wave my hand in front of his face. Saying, "Hello is anyone home?" I waved once more. Sally started laughing so hard, she couldn't speak. She coughed and giggled instead. Eric finally came to his senses and started to pull his hair. While whispering, "I can't believe it." "I can't believe it!" "That was the bravest thing I've ever seen!" "Alex you're my hero", as he wrapped his arms around me. He let's go and starts dancing in circles with no music. I started to laugh and began telling them, "No one talks bad about my mom's lemonade". "This means war." Sally just growled and Eric smiled. I had a new idea and all I need is something to write on. Maybe a piece of cardboard, paper and crayons. Sally jumps up and yells, "Ooh, I have paper at my house!" Eric begins to say, "I have big crayons at my house!" I replied, "we could make a for sale sign." We could write Lemonade for sale ten cents. Sally screams, "Ice cream!" Then takes off running, to go get paper. Eric takes his broken skateboard and his wheel home, to get crayons. I ask my mom for a little stand because we would like to sell her lemonade for money, so we could buy ice cream. She agreed. She picks up a small table just big enough to hold a pitcher of lemonade and a sign. Ten minutes later, I see Eric riding on Sally's back holding crayons in his left hand and paper in his right. Screaming we got it! We got it! As she jogged with Eric on her back. Sally began to smile but I couldn't see her teeth. I began to focus more with my eyes, squinting as I stared at Sally. The closer she got, the more I stared. She said, "What?" "This is my new grill." "It's a football mouth piece silly." Eric began to growl like a bear and yelled, "Lemonade for sale!" At that moment Sally dropped Eric on the ground but he was still yelling, "Lemonade for sale!" "Lemonade!" We all smiled and began to color our sign. It was yellow paper with a red outline lettering with a picture of a lemon on it. It read, fresh lemonade for sale. Ten cents, today only. We hung the sign in front of stand and place it on the edge of the grass. I smiled and gave Eric his very first cup of lemonade. He ran up and down the street. His arms waving above his head, as he screamed,

"Woot!" "Woot!" "This is so good!" I began to sing f-r-e-s-h lemonade t-o-d-a-y, o-n-l-y to-d-a-y. Sally was doing cartwheels behind me with her weird mouthpiece, shoulder pads and no shoes. I still can't believe she wears that all the time. Tommy was across the street. He had both of his thumbs in his ears and his four fingers wiggling in the air with his tongue out. He had a super long line of kids waiting to buy a cup of lemonade. I screamed, "Get your lemonade here for ten cents a cup!" "Today only!" Then all of the kids came running over to my stand. They could buy three times more lemonade for the price of one. I began to poke out my tongue and put both of my thumbs in each ear. Then wiggled my four fingers back and forth at the neighborhood bully. I turned around and took a deep breath. My heart was beating fast as I walked back to then lemonade stand. I began to think, what was going to happen to me later in the day. I began to tell Eric, how Tommy became a bully. While Sally sold the lemonade. He asked a kid for a pencil but instead, he snatch it out of the kids hand during school. The kid got scared because Tommy was much bigger. He just stood there as Tommy began to yell at him and his hair was flying back. The other kids stood back in shock and took off running. No one ever said anything else about it. Eric began to wonder if the story was real or fake. I replied, "That's what I heard." The kids in the background were screaming and yelling, "I want two cups of lemonade!" There must have been twenty kids. I began to add up the costs. There was twenty kids, who wanted two cups a lemonade at ten cents apiece. That's a two dollar value. We need at least four dollars and fifty cents if each ice cream is one dollar and fifty cents each. I hear Sally singing lemonade for s-a-l-e. She starts to point across the street. She says, "Alex look!" Tommy was changing his sign. It read, lemonade for sale today only 5 cents. All of the kids in my line, ran to Tommy's stand across the street. It was dust everywhere, from all of the running. I looked up towards the sky and seen this light brown cloud coming straight at us. Eric looked at Sally and me. He yelled, "Cover the lemonade quick!" Sally jumped towards the magic container and knocked over the lemonade. I put my hand over my eyes and kneeled on the ground, shaking my head from left to right. Sally was covered with lemonade soon to become sticky. The container hung on her head. She began to lift it up slowly and she had lemons on her head surrounded with ice cubes. Eric started laughing, beating his knees with the palm of his hands. The right side then the left. He said, "You should have seen it!" "It was like slow motion!" "I wish I had a camera!" Sally started to laugh. I started to laugh although there was no more lemonade. We all looked toward Tommy's lemonade stand and realized there will be no ice cream for us today. Eric jumped back in the swimming pool. Sally began to pick up her mess. I replied, "I will be right back."

I ran through the front door, leaving it opened. I headed to the stairway, skipping every other step on my way up. I made it to my room and grabbed my pillow. I turned around and ran back towards the stairway and begin to laugh as I look down at the steps. I jumped on the railing and slid down. I hopped off just before the end. Sprinting through the door, I began to yell, "Pillow fight!" While running, I smacked Eric in his head with the pillow. He dived under water. Still running. I ran towards Sally and hit her on the shoulder pads. The pillow burst and all the feathers flew out. Covering Sally from head to toe. I had forgot she was sticky from the lemonade. Now she looked like a football chicken as I stared and laughed. She began to run but none of the feathers were coming off. Sally ran towards Eric growling like a bear. Just when, Eric came up for air, she roared. Eric screamed so loud. He jumped out of the swimming pool and began to run while crying. Screaming and hollering. He must have ran about ten laps around the pool. I never laughed so hard before. I had knots in my stomach and I couldn't breathe. Sally stopped chasing Eric because she was laughing so hard. Eric started to notice, it was Sally who was chasing him. He grabbed his chest in relief while laughing. He replied, "Sally you look like a big furry chicken", as he continued to laugh. While Sally and Eric was laughing. I had a new idea. I began to think out loud, maybe we could have Sally become a mascot for Tommy. Eric replied, "Are you crazy!" "That's a bully!" I started to say, the ice cream truck will be here soon and we have only have two dollars. We need two dollars and fifty cents more. Sally wasn't into the idea but she wanted ice cream really bad.

We stood together, looking across the street. I had a worried look on my face. Eric put his right hand over his forehead looking down at the ground and Sally had her hands on her hips looking like a football chicken. I swallowed my pride. I looked both ways, starting from left to right before crossing the street. I wanted to make sure, no cars was coming. Tommy began looking at me. My heart began to jump out of my chest. I was scared. Once I reached the other side. I slowly approach Tommy with my hand out, to shake his hand. In my yard, Sally and Eric covered both of their eyes. Only leaving a small crack to see through. "Uh no.", they replied at the same time. Tommy begins to reach out, to shake my hand. I smiled because he was known as the neighborhood bully. This isn't supposed to happen. I thought to myself, what about the mean faces? We shook hands and introduce each other. I replied, "Hi, my name is Alex." "What's your name?" He said, "Tommy Hamburger." I replied, "Like the food burger?" "Yes", he said. He begun to laugh, so I started to laugh. In a loud voice, I called Sally and Eric over to meet him. He wasn't a bad person at all. Sally and Eric began to walk across the street, looking both ways before they cross. Tommy met them at the sidewalk and introduced himself. Hi, my name is Tommy. Eric's body began to wiggle and shake. It seemed like he had to use the bathroom really bad. Sally and I started to giggle. Eric just looked at him with big bubble eyes. Terrified as he stared. Sally spoke up. "Hi Tommy", she replied. Eric finally began to speak. He said, "What happened to being a bully at school?"

As he kept wiggling and talking like a mouse. He began to explain. While at school, I asked someone for a pencil. When the kid began to reach in his book bag and get a pencil. He reached out and dropped it on the ground. I bent over to pick it up and he stepped on my hand. I screamed really loud as I began to stand up. I screamed in his face. That's how I became known as a bully. The other kids are afraid of me. I'm glad to meet all of you because I have no friends. He said, "Would you like to help me sell lemonade?" We could split the money between us all and buy ice cream. Sally, Eric and I smiled. Eric began licking his lips. I began to daydream about ice cream with bubble gum eyes. That sweet taste when you bite into bubble gum. All that sugar, just makes me smile. "Yummy!" Sally started making noise like a chicken. Flapping her elbows up and down. Moving her neck forward and backwards screaming ice cream for s-a-l-e. Tommy was laughing so hard, he fell on the ground knees first. His face turned bright red like Santa's cheeks. With a smile on my face. I yelled, "Let's sell some lemonade!" One cup after another was being sold. The kids in the neighborhood loved the fact that Sally was a lemonade chicken with feathers. They just kept coming back for more lemonade. After selling the last cup of lemonade, we began to count all the money. Before we met Tommy, we had two dollars and fifty cents but now there is four of us today. We need three dollars and fifty cents more if we all want ice cream.

Tommy began to count as we crossed our fingers. Three dollars. Three dollars and a quarter. Three dollars and fifty cents. He jumped up with both arms in the air. He screamed, "We have it!" "We have enough for ice cream!" The rest of us jumped up and started dancing. Eric was jumping up and down. Sally started flapping her arms. Tommy high fived Eric and I was stomping my feet yelling ice cream! We began to split the money up between us, a dollar and fifty cents apiece. Then from a distance we hear music. We all looked at each other with our mouths open. The sound is getting louder and louder. We stood up and began to run towards the sound around the block. There it was, the ice cream truck. It was blue in color with pictures of different ice cream bars. It had a glow behind it from the sun. We were in heaven. We approached the truck and began our order. Tommy ordered an ice cream shaped like a taco. Sally ordered a chocolate cookie sandwich. Eric ordered a chocolate banana pop and I ordered a bird ice cream bar with bubble gum eyes. I ripped open the package to take my first bite of the bubble gum and began to chew. I stored the first piece in my cheek. It was so good, I bit the second piece and joined it with the first piece. Now I had one big piece of gum.

The ice cream began to drip down on the ground because it was hot outside. I began to eat faster, getting a brain freeze. I closed my eyes to warm my brain. I put my hand on my head and dropped my ice cream. I stared at the hot ground with my mouth wide open. Watching the ice cream melt into a milkshake. I couldn't believe it. This is what I worked for all day. I began to think, at least I still have my gum. I shrugged my shoulders and began smacking my lips as I walked away. "This gum is delicious", I said. The others were eating their ice cream as if they never ate before. They were a mess. Tommy had chocolate all over his mouth, nose and hands. Sally had cookies in her hair, not to mention feathers from my pillow. Eric had a chocolate and banana ear. We all laughed. Staying safe, we all walked home together saying our goodbyes for the day. My yard was a mess. I had a cooler, cups, lemonade peels, a ripped up pillow and feathers to pick up. I took a deep breath and began to clean up my mess. What a fun day. I thought to myself. Until tomorrow, we will see what happens.

Printed in the United States
by Baker & Taylor Publisher Services